This journal
belongs to:

 **SUMMER**
McKINNY

with a little help
from Clare Hutton

American Girl®

Wednesday, September 10

Aunt Olivia sent me this awesome journal from my favorite store, Makers & Bakers. It's her store! She sells craft supplies and kitchen gadgets for people who love to cook and make stuff—like me!

It's cool that she's in charge. I would LOVE to be my own boss someday. Since Aunt Olivia owns the store, she chooses everything she sells in it. I can tell she chose this journal just for me because I love lots of color.

I also love to bake. So does my sister, Holly. My whole family likes to be creative in the kitchen. Dad is our main chef. He experiments with recipes and ingredients from all over the world. Mom helps by slicing and dicing or mixing and rolling.

Baking is one thing Holly and I agree on. Mostly, we like different things.

Me → SISTERS, SIDE BY SIDE ← Holly

Me	Holly
Birthday	**Birthday**
June 21, 2015	December 21, 2013
(the first day of summer)	(the first day of winter)
Nickname	**Nickname**
Vacation	Mistletoe
Favorite food	**Favorite food**
Tacos (the kind with the crunchy shells)	Pizza (with loads of olives and mushrooms)
Favorite sweet treat	**Favorite sweet treat**
Cupcakes	Brownies
Favorite color	**Favorite color**
Rainbow!	Forest green
Favorite animal	**Favorite animal**
Dog	Owl
	(Holly keeps asking if we can have one as a pet.)
Favorite things to do	**Favorite things to do**
Play with dogs, ride my scooter, make crafts, camp, bake	Draw, paint, swim, read, bake
Favorite subject in school	**Favorite subject in school**
Science	Art

Aunt Olivia also sent me these cute stickers. She knows how much I love dogs, especially MY dog:

CRESCENT!!

I have ALWAYS wanted a dog. I've asked for one every birthday and Christmas. My parents FINALLY changed their no to a maybe, but they said I had to prove I was ready. So I made a list of everything a dog needs:

- Food
- Water
- Exercise
- Training
- Grooming
- Vet visits
- LOVE

I also did my chores without complaining for a month:

- Load the dishwasher
- Clean room
- Make bed
- Empty trash

Mom and Dad agreed I was ready, and our whole family went to Four Paws Animal Shelter. Even though I'm the one who wanted a dog most of all, we agreed everyone in the family would help take care of it.

All the dogs were SUPER cute, but I knew when I found MY dog. Whenever I talked, he tilted his head like he was thinking about what I was saying. When I got to hold him, he rested his head on my shoulder and fell asleep. I named him Crescent, because when he curls up, he looks just like a crescent roll.

I met a volunteer at the shelter named Fiona. She's a college student studying to be a veterinarian. I'm too young to volunteer at Four Paws, but Fiona got permission for me to help her there twice a month.

Crescent is almost a year old now, and Dad and I have trained him to follow basic commands. He's still working on "stay" (he wants to go where I go) and "drop it" (he loves to fetch his ball but doesn't like to give it back).

I'd love to get a doggy sibling (or two!) for Crescent, but Mom and Dad think one dog is enough.

MY FAMILY

Dad's a carpenter—he can build anything.

Mom LOVES math— she's an accountant.

Aunt Olivia is Dad's younger sister. Check out her measuring spoon necklace!

Me!

Crescent, the best boy in the world

Holly's almost 12, a year and a half older than me

Mom's leaving for a work trip on Saturday, and she'll be gone for five weeks. The good news is that Aunt Olivia, who lives in Baltimore, is coming to our house in Columbia. She stays with us whenever Mom or Dad travels. Aunt Olivia calls these visits Extra **Epic Sleepovers!** After school and on the weekends, she does baking and craft projects with me and Holly. It's way more fun than homework or chores (but we still have to do those, too).

Maryland

Columbia

Baltimore

Friday, September 12

It's Family Fun Friday. Every week, after school and work, we all go bike riding or paint pottery or do something else fun as a family. This week, we're making Aunt Olivia's favorite meal: fettuccine alfredo and lemon cupcakes. She'll be here by dinnertime!

Holly and I made a welcome sign. Then we decorated the cupcakes using the icing techniques Aunt Olivia taught us the last time she stayed with us. I couldn't wait to show her how good I'd gotten at making frosting flowers.

Holly wrote this part!

I wrote this part!

While Holly made the frosting, I pretended to be the host of my favorite baking show. "Can you tell our viewers what you're doing?" I asked, holding the spoon like a microphone.

Holly talked into the spoon. "I'm putting the frosting into piping bags so we can decorate the cupcakes. Meanwhile, my assistant is cleaning up." She looked at my side of the counter. "It's seriously a mess, Vacation." (That's her nickname for me.)

Aunt Olivia's favorite flower AND the state flower of Maryland

I said, "It's not that bad, Mistletoe." (That's my nickname for her.) "And who said I'm your assistant?" I used my baking show voice again to explain how to decorate the cupcake to look like a black-eyed Susan.

When the doorbell rang I couldn't wait to surprise Aunt Olivia with the fancy cupcakes. But she had a bigger surprise for us. Much bigger. She had a cat!

"This is Fettuccine," she said, setting a pet carrier in the front hall. "I adopted him a few weeks ago."

Dad didn't look happy, but Mom said it would be okay.

I wasn't so sure. Crescent had never met a cat before. Dad must have thought the same thing because he told me to put Crescent in the backyard. I led Crescent away, but I was confused. This is his house. Is he going to have to stay in the backyard for five weeks?

When I came back into the living room, Aunt Olivia was opening the door of the carrier. The fluffy white cat stepped out nervously and looked around. Holly tried to pet him, but he hissed and dashed under the couch. Aunt Olivia said Fettuccine needs some time to get used to our house. So we ate dinner on the patio and left the cat to explore.

Aunt Olivia MADE these for us! A dog for me and a unicorn for Holly.

Crescent was thrilled we were all outside. When he stood next to Aunt Olivia and wagged his tail, she said she was surprised at how much he had grown. Dad asked if she was still scared around big dogs.

I dropped my fork. Aunt Olivia is afraid of dogs?!

She said she wasn't afraid—just a little nervous sometimes. She patted Crescent, but she pulled back when he tried to lick her hand. I can't understand how anyone would be nervous around Crescent. He's such a sweet boy.

Except when someone steals his bed.

That's exactly what we found when we went inside. Fettuccine had come out from under the couch and made himself at home on CRESCENT'S bed. Crescent went NUTS. He started barking and ran toward Fettuccine, who zipped back under the couch.

Mom caught hold of Crescent's collar and pulled him away. She suggested Aunt Olivia keep Fettuccine in her room until the animals got used to each other. Aunt Olivia said she'd try, but she warned us that Fettuccine can be an escape artist.

After Aunt Olivia took Fettuccine upstairs, Holly said I should be happy because I've always wanted more pets.

WRONG. I want more DOGS. Why does my favorite aunt have to be a cat person?

Saturday, September 13

We all got up early to say goodbye to Mom. I hate it when she's gone for so long. But she promised she'd video-chat with us every night. Mom hugged me tight, and I didn't want to let go. Even Crescent leaned against Mom's legs. He's going to miss her, too.

When we went back into the house, we found out Aunt Olivia wasn't kidding about Fettuccine being an escape artist. He was not upstairs in her bedroom. He was in the living room, on top of the bookcase. Everything went bonkers all at once.

- Crescent started barking.
- Fettuccine started hissing.
- Holly starting yelling at Crescent to stop barking.
- I kept telling Crescent "No" and "Sit." It was too loud for Crescent to hear me, so Dad put him outside. AGAIN.

Fettuccine wouldn't come down from the bookcase, so Aunt Olivia went into the kitchen and came back shaking a bag of cat treats. Fettuccine jumped down in an instant and plopped to the floor by Aunt Olivia's feet. Then I

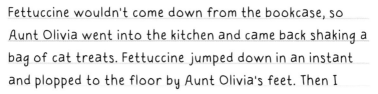

watched him get a treat for tormenting Crescent out of his own living room. UNBELIEVABLE!

I went to check on Crescent, and when I came back, Holly and Aunt Olivia were PLAYING with Fettuccine. Aunt Olivia asked if Crescent was okay, but Holly didn't seem interested in our dog. She was dangling a rainbow-colored puff from a string and laughing when Fettuccine batted at it. Aunt Olivia told Holly that she was a natural cat person.

I glared at Holly. Since when did she like cats? And why does our dog have to stay outside? IT'S NOT FAIR!

Sunday, September 14

Now that there's a cat in the house, I need to teach Crescent hand signals so he'll know what I want him to do even if he can't hear me.

Dad and I took him to the park for some training. We started Crescent with "sit," which he already knows. I put a treat in my hand and held out my hand flat and then raised it, saying "sit" at the same time. Crescent sat down. We practiced a bunch of times, until he would sit down without me saying anything, just watching my hand. He's so smart!

Our neighbor, Mrs. Li, was at the playground with her two kids and their papillon, Pixel, who is Crescent's BEST dog friend. Since Mrs. Li was pushing her little boys on the swings, I offered to play with her dog, too. We've taken care of Pixel when the Lis were on vacation, so she said yes right away.

Pixel

I heard Mrs. Li tell Dad she was impressed by how good I was with dogs. She wished she had time to give Pixel that much exercise every day. That's when I got an AMAZING IDEA.

I could be a dog walker! I could walk Pixel after school when I walk Crescent. The dogs would have fun and so would I!

Mrs. Li thought it was a great idea. Dad said it was a big responsibility. He agreed to let me try it for a few weeks, but he had some rules:

- Plan a route and stick to it so Mrs. Li knows where I am.
- Keep both dogs on their leashes at all times.
- Pack a bag of supplies.
- Bring a cell phone in case I need help.

I couldn't wait to tell Aunt Olivia I had a job! She was excited for me, and she reminded me and Dad that she would be close by if I needed anything.

When I started drawing a map of my route, Holly looked over my shoulder and tried to tell me which way to go. I told her it was none of her business. It's MY business. A dog-walking business. And I start tomorrow!

Monday, September 15

I was so excited about my dog-walking adventure that it was impossible to pay attention in school. I didn't want to memorize state capitals when I had cute dogs to think about.

The BEST boy!

Crescent was eager for our walk!

Crescent was waiting at the door when I got home, and we headed to the laundry room for my dog-walking backpack. When I turned the light on, I almost screamed. Fettuccine was on the dryer, lying on top of my backpack. How the heck did he get out of Aunt Olivia's room?

I closed the door so Crescent wouldn't see the cat.
"Shoo!" I said, but Fettuccine just blinked at me. I didn't
want to try picking him up, so I grabbed a dirty sock and
tossed it into the corner. Crescent would have run after
that, but Fettuccine didn't move.

My backpack
is under his
butt!

It was my first day on the job and I was NOT
going to let that cat make me late! After a
moment, Fettuccine stood up and stretched and
I was able to grab my backpack. I dashed out
of the room, shutting the cat inside.

My backpack has poop bags,
dog treats, a collapsible water bowl,
water, a phone, hand sanitizer,
and a tennis ball.

Our walk was great! Pixel and Crescent had fun together, and I LOVED playing with them both.

It went so well that I wished I had even MORE dogs to take care of!

Pixel likes to run under Crescent's belly. Crescent always looks so confused!

We dropped off Pixel, and I was in SUCH a good mood when I got home. At least I was until I saw Holly and Aunt Olivia playing with Fettuccine in the living room—AGAIN. I thought he was supposed to stay in Aunt Olivia's room!

Crescent started to bark, and Fettuccine arched his back and hissed at Crescent.

"Sorry," Aunt Olivia said, grabbing Fettuccine. "I'll take him upstairs."

She carried him away, and Holly frowned at me. She said I should put Crescent out in the yard so they could keep playing with Fettuccine. She thinks it's not fair that Fettuccine has to stay in Aunt Olivia's room all the time.

"He doesn't!" I said. "He sneaks out all the time." I told her about finding Fettuccine in the laundry room. "It's not fair for Crescent to be outside all the time. Go up to Aunt Olivia's room if you want to play with the cat."

Without saying another word, Holly went upstairs. I couldn't believe it! She took Fettuccine's side. Holly and Aunt Olivia only seemed interested in that cat.

Tuesday, September 16

Aunt Olivia had a surprise for us after school—and it didn't have anything to do with cats. It was a new cookie recipe! We put on some music and danced around the kitchen, talking and laughing and having a Great Bake Break. (That's what Aunt Olivia calls it.) We made raspberry macarons with chocolate cream filling. I called them MACARO-MAZING.

I was eating my third cookie when Crescent nudged my hand and looked at me with his big brown eyes, begging for a taste. I had to tell him no. Dogs can

get sick from chocolate. That's when I had an idea: dog cookies. We could have a Great Bake Break just for Crescent!

Lots of foods are poisonous to dogs, like grapes, raisins, onions, garlic, macadamia nuts, and avocados!

Holly said she'd rather do homework than make dog food, so she left. But Aunt Olivia was happy to help me search online for a recipe. There were so many! We finally chose one made with canned pumpkin and peanut butter that came from a veterinarian's website. Crescent doesn't have any food allergies, so we knew it was safe.

When Dad got home an hour later, there were ingredients all over the counter and a batch of dog cookies cooling on the stove. He picked one up and said, "New recipe?"

"Dad, WAIT!!" I shouted.

But it was too late. He took a big bite. Aunt Olivia started laughing and I cracked up, too. Dad ate a DOG treat! His face turned bright red, but all he said was, "Interesting."

While Dad started making lasagna, I put the dog cookies in a container. They did smell good. I thought if Dad could try one, so could I.

NEWS FLASH: DOG COOKIES DO NOT TASTE GOOD IF YOU'RE NOT A DOG.

At dinner I told Dad again how great it had been to walk two dogs. In fact, it had been so much fun that all I'd been thinking about was adding ANOTHER dog. Mr. Rosario, who lives down the street, has an older labradoodle named Thor. Thor and Pixel are friends, and Thor and Crescent sniff hello whenever they see each other. Thor would be a great addition to our walks.

Aunt Olivia thought it was a good idea, but Dad said we had to make sure Thor and Crescent got along. So Dad invited Thor and Mr. Rosario to our house. The grown-ups sat on the patio while I played with the dogs in the yard.

The dogs got along great, but something weird happened when Thor tried to say hello to Aunt Olivia. He put his paw on her arm (Thor loves to shake) and Aunt Olivia FROZE. Then she quickly took a step back, and Thor dropped his paw.

A labradoodle is a mix of Labrador retriever and poodle.

24

I guess she wasn't kidding when she said she was nervous around big dogs.

Before Thor and Mr. Rosario left, I showed Mr. Rosario the list of ingredients for the dog cookies and asked if Thor could have one. Thor gobbled it up. Mr. Rosario said he'd already decided to hire me to walk Thor. He said now he was thinking about hiring me to bake for Thor!

DOG TREAT INGREDIENTS
whole wheat flour, eggs, canned pumpkin, natural peanut butter, water, cinnamon, salt

Back inside I started cheering. "I have TWO clients. I'm in business!"

Holly said, "Having a job isn't the same thing as having a business, Vacation."

I said, "How would you know, Mistletoe?"

But Aunt Olivia said I have what it takes to be a good business owner because I'm passionate about what I'm doing.

I could tell Holly was a little jealous. But later, when I went upstairs, I heard Holly in Aunt Olivia's room. They were playing with Fettuccine and laughing together. I felt totally left out. I know Aunt Olivia likes cats more than dogs. Does she like Holly better than me now that Holly's a cat person?

Wednesday, September 17

Today was my day to help at Four Paws, the animal shelter where we adopted Crescent.

Fiona and I started by cleaning the outdoor dog runs. I told her all about my dog-walking business, and Fiona said she was proud of me.

Cleaning cat cages was next, and one of the cats started meowing the moment we walked in the room. Fiona said it was Daphne, who talks to everyone. I went over to her cage, and the gray cat rubbed her face against the door and purred. Then she stuck her paw out and patted my hand. She's way friendlier than Fettuccine!

Daphne has been at the shelter for over a month. Fiona said lots of people want kittens, but they're not as interested in an older cat. I'm no cat person, but I think Daphne's really sweet.

An iguana named Tiger

Daphne and lots of other cats

A rabbit

Two guinea pigs (Fiona says these have to be adopted together. They get lonely.)

Lots of dogs, some seem very nervous.

I helped Fiona take inventory in the supply room. The shelter depends on donations to help take care of all the animals. While we were counting bags of cat litter, I realized now that I'm making my own money, I can use some of it to buy supplies for Four Paws! Then I could help even more animals with my business.

Four Paws Animal Shelter

DONATIONS

Thursday, September 18

> Walking three dogs was AWESOME!

It was also very, very busy.

- Pixel ran after EVERY squirrel she saw.
- Thor got tired and lay down whenever he felt like it.
- Crescent pooped. No surprise, but the poop bags were still in my backpack. Getting those out, while holding a leash in each hand, wasn't easy. (At least no one went home with poop on their paws.)

By the time we finished our walk, I was exhausted from the dogs tugging on their leashes. Aunt Olivia made me a fruit smoothie and asked how it felt to be the boss. I told her I got pulled in a lot of directions at once. She told me not to be afraid to ask for help, which was sort of confusing. Aren't the dogs <u>my</u> responsibility?

Aunt Olivia said it's also responsible to let people know you need help. She owns her store, but she hires people to help run it. And Mom and Dad ask for her help when one of them has to travel for work. Aunt Olivia said if I ever need to leave Crescent home while I walk the other dogs, she'd be happy to watch him.

Okaaaaay. But Aunt Olivia is NOT a dog person. When I mentioned that, Aunt Olivia said she cares about Crescent, even though she doesn't want her own dog. "He's my dog nephew."

That made me laugh. "Does that mean Fettuccine is my cat cousin?"

Aunt Olivia grinned. "Family's family, whether you have two legs or four."

Friday, September 19

Aunt Olivia is staying overnight in Baltimore to do some work at her store. She took Fettuccine with her. After they left, Crescent searched Aunt Olivia's room, sniffing. He seemed to know the cat was gone. Holly said she missed Fettuccine already, but I was glad Crescent could go anywhere he wanted in the house again.

Dad announced that Family Fun Friday would be a campout in the backyard. While he grilled barbecued chicken, Holly and I sat on our sleeping bags and made friendship bracelets. After dinner, we did our nightly video chat with Mom. We toasted marshmallows over the fire while Mom ate marshmallows out of a bag in her hotel room. Crescent wiggled his way between Dad's and my sleeping bags, and I felt like our family was all together again.

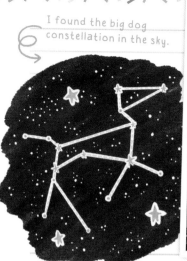
I found the big dog constellation in the sky.

I told everyone what Aunt Olivia had said about
Fettuccine being my cousin. Mom and Dad laughed, but
Holly said that I wasn't a very good cousin because
I hadn't even tried to play with Fettuccine and I let
Crescent bark at him.

WHAT?! I told Holly she wasn't a very good sister because
she always takes Fettuccine's side. Crescent is OUR dog
and this is HIS home. It's not fair that he always gets
scolded or sent outside because of a cat that doesn't
even LIVE here.

Holly said she didn't feel like camping out anymore and
stormed inside. Family Fun Friday was over, and it was all
Fettuccine's fault. Even when he's not here, that cat ruins
everything.

Saturday, September 20

Holly and I still weren't talking to each other when Aunt Olivia and Fettuccine got back from Baltimore today. But when Aunt Olivia invited us into her room to teach us how to knit, we both said yes.

She told us knitting isn't hard.

NEWS FLASH: KNITTING IS HARD.

You have to hold a stick in each hand and use one to tie yarn around the other. I just couldn't get my fingers to work right. It seemed to take forever to "cast on"—to make the first line of stitches. Aunt Olivia is making a sweater, but I need to start with something easier, like a blanket.

That made me think of Four Paws. The shelter puts blankets in the cages to comfort the animals. Could I make a blanket for them? When I mentioned it, Holly said I'm so slow that all the animals will get adopted before I finish one blanket.

Aunt Olivia said I could make small squares instead. It would be easier, and she would sew them together to make a blanket. Holly even said she'd help, so we each started on a square. My yarn kept tangling, and Holly told me to pull it tighter. She acted like she's been knitting her

whole life! I was about to tell her to mind her own business when there was a tug at my yarn, and the whole ball disappeared under the bed.

FETTUCCINE!!

I glanced at Holly. Last night she'd said that I never play with the cat. This was my chance. I pulled the yarn back, slooooowwwly dragging it across the floor, and he POUNCED! He rolled around, wrapping the yarn around his body and kicking with his back paws. When I dangled the yarn above him, Fettuccine leaped high into the air, twisting his body but landing perfectly on his feet. Back on the ground, he crouched low and stared at the yarn that I was pulling back and forth. Holly and I started laughing when he wiggled his butt and ran after the yarn.

I guess my little kitty cousin isn't all bad.

Monday, September 22

It's dog-walking day! I'd been thinking about what Aunt Olivia had said about asking for help, so before school, I went into Holly's room. She showed me the new picture she's working on of an owl taking off from a tree branch. It's so detailed, and she's painting the feathers with a dozen different shades. I said it looked "owl-some."

I asked Holly if she would help me walk the dogs. I expected her to say yes right away, but she hesitated. She wanted to work on her picture, not spend all afternoon at the dog park. I don't know why anyone would choose drawing over dogs, but when Holly starts a new art project, she gets obsessed. She finally said she'd help me if I paid her half the money.

I said, "FINE!"

But it was NOT fine. On the walk, Holly wanted to make ALL the decisions.

After one walk, I'm not sure if having Holly's know-it-all help is worth it.

Having her with me did make some things easier, though:
1. I held only Pixel's leash, so it didn't get tangled with the others when Pixel took off after squirrels.
2. When Thor stopped to rest, Holly stayed with him.
3. Crescent wasn't jealous when I paid attention to the other dogs.

Tuesday, September 23

I had big news to share at dinner tonight. My teacher, Mrs. DeClemente, told us about a local business fair for kids. It's a day to sell anything we want—as long as we make it ourselves. We get to keep the money we make, AND there are three cash prizes!

Holly said she hoped I wasn't planning to knit anything. Ha. Ha. I'm planning to make dog treats! If I can have a dog-walking business, I can have a dog treat business, too. And I can donate some of the money I make to Four Paws to help even more animals.

Aunt Olivia said it was a great opportunity. She said we are a family of bakers and makers, and we can work together!

One problem: The rules say kids have to do the work themselves. I can't let anyone else make the dog cookies. But that's okay. I WANT to make them. I also want to come up with a fun name for my business. Here are my ideas:

MUTTS ABOUT MY PUP!

- ~~Dog Days with Summer~~
- Barks & Biscuits
- Pupsy Daisy
- Pup Cakes
- Desserts for Dogs
- ~~Give a Dog a Bone~~
- Summer's Dog Snacks
- Woofs and Wags
- Waggy Pup Tails

Dad was reading the rules of the fair online, and he said kids can sell goods <u>and</u> services. Aunt Olivia suggested I make flyers about my dog-walking service to hand out at the fair. She called that "advertising." We brainstormed all the things I could offer.

- Walks
- Extra playtime
- Feeding
- Bathing
- Brushing and combing
- Help with training

We also talked about other things that could make my business special:

- Use cute dog-shaped cookie cutters.
- Package the dog cookies in pretty bags with rainbow ribbons.
- Include the ingredient list on every bag, so owners can check for anything their dog might be allergic to.

Aunt Olivia said I had a great business model (whatever that is). But Dad was worried that I was going to have way too much work for one person.

I looked at Holly. "I could do this if I had help," I said. "Please, Mistletoe? I know you want a new set of pastel paint pens. If you help me walk the dogs, you'd make enough money to buy them. Please?"

That did it. Holly said yes.

Dad helped me fill out the application for the fair, and I told Mom all about it when we video-chatted. She was really excited and said, "Paws crossed you get in!"

Wednesday, September 24

When Holly and I got back from walking the dogs,
Fettuccine was out. As in OUTSIDE. On our front porch!

Crescent yanked the leash right out of my hand and
charged. Fettuccine yowled and dashed away with
Crescent close behind.

I ran after Crescent, and Holly ran after Fettuccine.
I caught Crescent, but Holly came back empty-handed.

When we told Aunt Olivia what happened, she got really
scared. She didn't even know Fettuccine had gotten
outside. She said we HAD to find him. Holly and I split up
to search the neighborhood while Aunt Olivia looked
around the yard.

I searched and searched, getting more and more worried.
I was starting to panic when I saw a blur of white fur
dash into a bush. I dropped to my
knees and peered under the
branches. It was Fettuccine!
But I couldn't reach him.

I slipped off my friendship
bracelet and started wiggling
it in front of Fettuccine. He watched
and crept ever so slowly toward me
as I trailed it along the ground. When he was close
enough, I grabbed him and put him in the carrier I'd
brought with me.

At home, Holly yelled at me, saying it was my fault because
I hadn't trained Crescent. That made me so MAD! I yelled
back. "It's not Crescent's fault that Fettuccine keeps
escaping! The cat is the troublemaker!"

Aunt Olivia looked like she was about to cry and said
Fettuccine doesn't like being stuck in one room.

Now I feel terrible. Even if what I said was true, I had
hurt my aunt's feelings. What if Aunt Olivia and
Fettucine go home to Baltimore?

Thursday, September 25

I tossed and turned all night worrying that Aunt Olivia would leave. I got up early and saw that the light was on in her room. I knocked, and when I went in, Aunt Olivia was setting a bowl of cat food on the floor. Fettuccine started to eat, and I couldn't believe what my aunt did next. She grabbed a bunch of fur at his neck and stuck a NEEDLE into him!

Aunt Olivia explained that Fettuccine has DIABETES! She has to give him a shot of insulin every day. That's why she had to bring him with her to our house. She said, "He trusts me to give him the shot, but I'm not sure he'd let anyone else do it."

And that's why Aunt Olivia got so scared when he ran away yesterday. Fettuccine doesn't know our neighborhood, so he could have gotten lost. If he went too many days without his insulin, he could get really, really sick.

After he ate, Aunt Olivia picked up Fettuccine, and he started purring. I asked if it was scary to give him a shot. I couldn't imagine sticking Crescent with a

needle every day! Aunt Olivia said she was nervous at first—she didn't want to hurt Fettuccine. But the vet taught her that Fettuccine wouldn't even notice if he was distracted with food. "Now we're both used to the shot."

Fettuccine looked calm and even cuddly. I reached my hand out, and after he sniffed my fingers, I scratched him gently under his chin. He closed his eyes and leaned into my hand. "I'm sorry you need shots," I told Fettuccine.

I didn't even know cats could get diabetes. I feel bad that living here has been stressful for Fettuccine. I HAVE to make things better.

Friday, September 26

Holly bailed on helping me walk the dogs. Instead, she stayed after school for Art Club. I was going to ask Aunt Olivia for help, but she left me a message saying she'd gotten a flat tire. She'd be home as soon as it was fixed.

I didn't want to be late for my job, so I put Crescent in the backyard. He whimpered when I left, but I knew it would be easier walking the other two dogs without him. I PROMISED Crescent he'd get a walk next.

Thor and Pixel missed Crescent, and I did, too. Crescent must have missed us, because when I got home, he was barking

like crazy. As soon as I got to the backyard, I told him to be quiet, but he didn't listen. That's when I saw Fettuccine sitting in the window in Aunt Olivia's room. I clipped Crescent's leash to his collar. He needed to get away from that cat.

I took Crescent for an extra long walk. Dad and Holly were back when I got home, and Dad was on the phone. I heard him saying, "This afternoon? That's weird, he doesn't usually bark much. No, it won't happen again, I'll make sure of it. Sorry you were disturbed."

When Dad hung up, he told me Mr. Wylie, whose house is behind ours, called to complain about Crescent's barking. Dad said I should NEVER leave Crescent alone in the yard when no one is home. I said it was Holly's fault. She didn't keep her promise to help me.

Holly said she never wanted to walk the dogs but that I had BEGGED her to. Dad said we were both responsible and that we had to figure out a way to make things work. If we couldn't, then no more dog-walking business and no more Art Club. Holly said, "Thanks a lot, Summer!" and stormed up to her room.

Dad ordered pizza and Aunt Olivia made ice cream sundaes for Family Fun Friday, but no one had much fun. Holly and I didn't even look at each other.

Saturday, September 27

When Aunt Olivia took Holly to swim practice, I asked Dad if he knew that Fettuccine has diabetes. He said he didn't find out until after Aunt Olivia arrived. Since Fettuccine needs Aunt Olivia's help, and we need Aunt Olivia's help, Dad said we have to make the best of it. I told Dad I'd work on helping Crescent and Fettuccine get along better.

I felt bad that Crescent had bothered Mr. Wylie, so I asked Dad if I could make the neighbor some cookies as an apology. Dad said it's ALWAYS a good idea to tell people how we feel, otherwise they won't know. "But just don't make him the dog cookies," Dad teased.

Crescent and I delivered the message, and Mr. Wylie laughed when he saw the sad dog faces. He said he forgave us AND that the cookies were delicious.

I knew I needed to apologize to someone else, too. I used some yarn from the blanket squares I was knitting to make a cat toy for Fettuccine. When I showed it to Aunt Olivia, she said Fettuccine would love it. "Let's give it to him," she said. We went to her room, and Aunt Olivia and I played with Fettuccine together. I liked watching Fettuccine with his new toy, but I really liked spending time with Aunt Olivia.

Sunday, September 28

I got in! I HAVE A SPOT IN THE BUSINESS FAIR! The event will take place outside, in Centennial Park. Aunt Olivia is almost as excited as I am! I'm going to have a table to display my dog treats, and I can decorate it however I want. Aunt Olivia has ideas for "merchandising," which means making my product noticeable.

Holly asked how many dog treats I was going to make. It was the first time she'd talked to me since Dad had scolded us. I just said, "A lot." I don't need Holly telling me I'm wrong again.

I have three weeks to get ready for the fair, and I'm SO excited. Aunt Olivia's going to take me shopping for supplies to package my dog cookies. Here's what I need:

- Bags
- Ribbon
- Stickers
- Paper

48

I'll also need to buy the ingredients for the cookies. Aunt Olivia said I should buy as many supplies as I can in bulk (that means large quantities) to save money.

I haven't spent any of the money I've made from my dog-walking business yet, but I'm not sure I'll have enough to buy everything I need. Aunt Olivia said she'll pay for whatever I can't afford and that I can pay her back after the business fair. Then she told me a bunch of stuff about "expenses."

- Keep track of everything I spend.
- After the fair, count the money I make.
- Subtract what I spent from what I made. That's my PROFIT.
- Decide how much of my profit I'm going to donate to the animal shelter.

I can't wait to talk to Mom about everything during our call tonight.

Monday, September 29

We got back from shopping to the sounds of howling
and hissing and raced upstairs. Crescent must have
managed to push Aunt Olivia's bedroom door open. He
had Fettuccine trapped on the top shelf of the closet.
Crescent was jumping at him, and Fettuccine looked scared!

Fettuccine had caused a lot of problems by escaping from his room. But today he'd stayed where he was supposed to be, and Crescent had come after him. This wasn't Fettuccine's fault at all!

I took Crescent out to the front porch so we could talk. Here's what I told him.

> We can't expect Fettuccine to stay in one room. It's not fair. He's used to having a whole house to live in—no wonder he keeps escaping.
> (Crescent tilted his head at me. He was listening!)

> Breaking into Fettuccine's room is NOT okay. He needs to feel safe in there. (Sad eyes from Crescent. I can tell he's sorry.)

> I'm working on becoming better friends with Fettuccine. I'm going to help you two get along better, too. After all, he's your kitty cousin! (Crescent barked excitedly.)

I know just the right person to talk to—Fiona!

Tuesday, September 30

There were new animals at the shelter today. Three cute
kittens, a friendly long-haired dog, and a ferret named
Potato Chip.

While Fiona and I washed food bowls, I explained everything
that had been going on. Fiona gave me GREAT advice:

- Put a pet gate at the door to Aunt Olivia's room. That
  way, Fettuccine and Crescent can see each other but
  won't be able to get to each other.
- Put Crescent on a leash so I can control him if he
  gets excited.
- Make sure the whole family works together to help the
  pets get along.

Fiona said the last tip was really important. Animal training
won't work if there's only one person doing it. She said
I need everyone's help. (I guess that means Holly, too.)

Before I left, I stopped in to see Daphne, who is still at the shelter. Fiona and I took Daphne into an adoption room so she could wander around and play. It's stressful for animals to be in cages all the time. Daphne sat in my lap purring, and I told her about trying

to help Fettuccine and Crescent get along. Before I put her back in her cage, Daphne rubbed her face against mine. I think that was her way of wishing me luck.

Aunt Olivia picked me up from the shelter, and on the way home we got the supplies we needed for OPERATION FRIENDSHIP. After we got the gate installed, I put Crescent on his leash and let him watch Holly and Aunt Olivia play with Fettuccine. Then Dad and I told Crescent to "come" and "stay," using the commands we'd practiced. Crescent was distracted, but when he listened, I gave him lots of praise and treats.

Holly asked if this would really work. I said once they're used to each other, Crescent won't chase Fettuccine and Fettuccine won't be scared. All Holly said was, "I guess we'll find out."

Thursday, October 9

We've done gate training with Fettuccine and Crescent every day for a week. There hasn't been any barking or hissing for a few days, so today we decided to try it without Crescent's leash.

Holly tossed a puff for Fettuccine to chase on their side of the gate, and I played tug-of-war with Crescent on our side. Everything was fine until Fettuccine's puff flew over the gate. Crescent barked and ran to the gate.

I said, "Sit, Crescent! Stay!"

AND HE DID! The training is working!

Afterward, I took Crescent and Pixel for a walk. Thor was at the vet, so I didn't expect Holly to help me since I only had two dogs. But she did because Dad told her she had to.

As soon as we got to the park, Pixel found a squirrel to chase. She tugged her leash right out of Holly's hand, and

Holly had to chase her. They started running circles around us. Pixel thought it was a game and made happy yipping sounds.

"Make her stop!" Holly said. "I'm getting dizzy."

I grabbed Pixel's leash and said, "Sit!" Pixel sat.

Holly said, "You're way better with dogs than I am, Vacation. That's why I didn't think it would be a big deal that I didn't help you walk them before."

I told Holly it was a big deal. She made me a promise and then she just ignored it.

Holly said she was sorry, and I could tell she meant it. When she said she wanted to make it up to me, Crescent and Pixel both started barking. That made me laugh. "It sounds like the dogs will give you another chance, so I will, too."

It was nice to know that Holly thought I was good at this.

Saturday, October 11

Aunt Olivia had a "business surprise" for me today. I was kinda confused when she led me to the driveway, but when Dad opened the garage door, I gasped. There was the cutest cart! Aunt Olivia uses it at Makers & Bakers and thought I could use it at the business fair.

This is going to be SO awesome! I asked Aunt Olivia if I could paint it, and Holly got all excited. She started telling me what I should do and what colors I should use.

But I wanted to use my ideas, not Holly's. Aunt Olivia said I should embrace my vision.

I spent an hour trying to draw my vision on paper, but I couldn't get it right. Finally, I asked Holly to help, and she said yes right away. Even better, she drew what I wanted, not what she thought it should be. When we finished designing the cart, Holly offered to help me design the Waggy Pup Tails logo. I said yes right away.

Aunt Olivia made a new canopy. (I picked the fabric!)

Dad built these cute shelves.

WAGGY PUP TAILS

Holly drew my logo on the front.

We added a chalkboard.

Sunday, October 12

I spent the morning in Aunt Olivia's room working on my blanket squares. Aunt Olivia worked on her sweater. Fettuccine worked on capturing our yarn. He kept dashing out from under the bed and then skittering away again. He was so funny and cute!

Aunt Olivia thanked me for working so hard to help Fettuccine and Crescent get along. I told her that I was sorry I wasn't a cat person. Then I confessed that when she first arrived, I felt really left out when she spent time with Fettuccine and Holly but not with me and Crescent.

Aunt Olivia gave me a hug and said she never meant to leave me out. Then she told me she was sorry she hadn't helped more with my dog-walking business. "Even though I'm nervous around big dogs, I'm sorry I let my dog nephew down. But I'm even more sorry I let my niece down."

I felt like a weight rolled off my shoulders. Dad was right. We need to tell people how we feel.

Tuesday, October 14

It's been almost a week since I took Crescent off his leash around Fettuccine, and there hasn't been any trouble. It's time for the next step.

We took down the gate!

While Aunt Olivia and Holly played with Fettuccine in Aunt Olivia's room, I called Crescent upstairs. He trotted right past Aunt Olivia's room and didn't even notice the gate was gone. I was petting him when Fettuccine came and sat in the open doorway.

Crescent stiffened. He and Fettuccine STARED at each other. I said, "Stay, Crescent," firmly, and kept petting him. My heart was pounding.

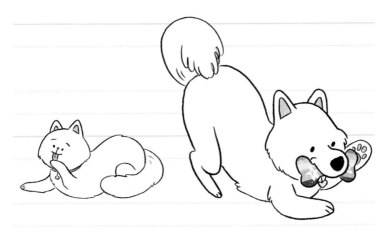

Crescent stayed, and Fettuccine looked away.

"Does this mean we don't need to keep Fettuccine shut in Aunt Olivia's room anymore?" Holly asked.

Aunt Olivia had a huge smile on her face. She said as long as someone's home, we can let Fettuccine roam around the house.

We did it!
OPERATION
FRIENDSHIP is
a success!!!

Wednesday, October 15

Aunt Olivia drove us to Four Paws after school so we could deliver the blanket we'd made. Fiona and I showed Aunt Olivia around. Daphne is still there. When she saw me, she meowed hello and started purring. Fiona let Aunt Olivia hold Daphne, and Holly scratched Daphne's ear while I set the blanket in Daphne's cage.

"She's a sweet cat, isn't she?" I said when she was back in her cage, kneading her paws on the blanket. Holly agreed.

Aunt Olivia picked up a long-handled cat toy and pretended to knight me by tapping it on each of my shoulders. "Summer McKinny, I declare you an official cat person."

Thursday, October 16

I was grooming Crescent today when Aunt Olivia said she had a gift for him. It turns out the rainbow sweater she's been knitting was for him! "It's a little something special for my favorite nephew," she said. "Thank you for sharing your house with my cat."

Crescent tried on the sweater right away. He looked VERY handsome. He's going to be the best dressed dog at the dog park this winter!

Friday, October 17

Everyone agreed to spend Family Fun Friday helping me get ready for the fair. It's TOMORROW!

After school, Holly offered to walk Crescent so that I could start making the dough. Aunt Olivia was in charge of taking the cookies out of the oven so I could focus on decorating them (once they'd cooled, of course). Dad came home, and we set up an assembly line for packaging and labeling the cookies with the list of ingredients. We played music and danced around the kitchen and had our first ever Great BARK Bake Break.

When I had everything packed up for the fair, Dad said he was impressed with everything I'd done. Aunt Olivia gave me a hug and said, "Way to go, boss!" Then Holly handed me a package wrapped in rainbow-colored paper. Inside was a T-shirt with the Waggy Pup Tails logo printed on it. I told her I'd look like a real business owner tomorrow, and she said I already was one. It felt really good to have my family behind me.

Saturday, October 18

The business fair was the coolest thing ever! Everyone had really unique displays. One girl used a tree in the park to hang her birdhouses, and another boy strung a clothesline between two lampposts to display his tie-dyed shirts. Kids were selling handmade soap, beaded bracelets, painted flowerpots, cupcakes and cookies, candles, key chains, and knitted hats and scarves. Daisy, a girl who goes to my school, had two six-foot-tall cat trees covered in handmade cat toys!

Crescent hung out by my cart, and lots
of people stopped to say hello to him.

There were so many people, and at first I was nervous
about answering questions from grown-ups. But I was
talking about my two favorite things—dogs and baking—
so it was really easy. Dad watched me wait on some
customers, and he said he was really proud of me.

Fiona came to the fair and bought four bags of dog cookies. She also had news. Daphne's been adopted! At first I felt sad. I won't get to see her again! But I was mostly happy that Daphne has a forever home now. Her new family is really lucky.

I was nervous when the judges came to my cart because I had to tell them about my business. They asked a lot of questions and they all liked meeting Crescent. "He's my inspiration," I explained. One judge said I looked very professional. I turned to see if Aunt Olivia had heard them, and that's when I saw MOM! She was home!

She wrapped her arms around me in a huge hug, and I squeezed her tight. I wanted to tell her every single thing that had happened today, but I still had work to do.

At the end of the fair, the judges gathered everyone

together and congratulated us for our hard work and creativity. Then it was time for the AWARDS! I held my breath. They called the winner for "best business potential," and everyone clapped as a boy even younger than me walked to the front of the crowd. And then I heard MY name.

I WON BEST PRESENTATION!

The judges said my cookies were beautifully decorated and packaged and that my display was bright and appealing. They said I also did a great job presenting my business to the judges and to my customers. My family cheered so loud as the judges handed me a certificate and a check for $500. That's going to help a lot of animals at the shelter. I felt so proud!

Today was amazing, but the best part was coming home with Mom and finding Fettuccine curled up in the middle of Crescent's dog bed. A few weeks ago, Crescent would have freaked out! But tonight he just walked over to Fettuccine and lay down next to him with a contented doggy sigh.

Sunday, October 19

Aunt Olivia and Fettuccine went back to Baltimore today. I'm going to miss them both. I think Fettuccine's going to miss Crescent. They ended up being pretty good friends.

Holly and I made three different kinds of muffins for our final breakfast with Aunt Olivia. Before we could eat, the doorbell rang, and Aunt Olivia announced that she had a present for Holly and me. "Your parents said it was okay."

We all went to the front hall, and when Dad opened the door, Fiona was standing there holding a pet carrier. I was completely confused until a little gray paw reached out.

It was DAPHNE!!!!

"This sweetie needs some cat people to be her family," Aunt Olivia said. "She's lived with dogs before, and now that Crescent has learned to get along with Fettuccine, he's going to LOVE Daphne."

Holly hugged Aunt Olivia while I scooped Daphne into my arms. Aunt Olivia put Crescent on his leash and kept him back, but Crescent's tail was wagging as he looked at Daphne.

Finally, another pet to love.

I need to look up cat treat recipes.

It's time for a **Great** PURR **Bake** Break!

WAGGY PUP TAILS COOKIES

Make your furry friend a batch of tasty treats. (Make sure your dog doesn't have any allergies to the ingredients.)

Ingredients

2½ cups whole wheat flour

2 eggs

½ cup pumpkin

2 tablespoons peanut butter

½ teaspoon salt

½ teaspoon ground cinnamon

Water, at least 1 teaspoon

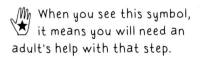 When you see this symbol, it means you will need an adult's help with that step.

Directions

Have an adult preheat the oven to 350°F. Line a baking sheet with parchment paper and set aside.

1. In a large bowl, stir together the flour, eggs, pumpkin, peanut butter, salt, and cinnamon.

2. Transfer the mixture onto the kitchen counter and knead with your hands until the mixture comes together. Add water if needed, 1 teaspoon at a time, until it's easy to squish but not gooey. The mixture should be dry and stiff.

3. Roll the dough out with a rolling pin to about ¼-inch thickness. Use cookie cutters to cut shapes, and place them on the prepared baking sheet.

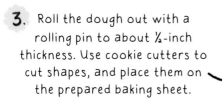

4. With help from an adult, bake at 350°F for 40 minutes. The treats should be golden brown and crunchy. Let cool before feeding to your dog.

Real Girl Entrepreneur

Entrepreneur *(on-truh-pruh-NUR)* A person who organizes and owns a business

Meet Anna B. She plays soccer, swims, does crafts, and likes shopping. Oh, and she owns her own business. It's called Artsy Anna, and the nine-year-old entrepreneur participated in her first business fair in her home state of Wisconsin.

What do you make?
Fancy cups. I use the Cricut machine to cut out stickers and decorate drinking cups.

What got you interested in doing this?
I like to do crafts. I paint and make T-shirts and bracelets. One day I saw a glass cup design and wanted to try making it myself.

How long does it take to make one item?
After the stickers are ready, it takes about ten minutes. Some cups take longer if they have a lot of colors.

I made 8 different cup designs and decorated 24 cups.

What inspires you when you are designing your items?
I like to look at Pinterest and find cute designs.

Have you participated in any kids' business fairs? When and where?
I just went to my first one—the Young Entrepreneurs Craft Fair at our public library.

Do you plan on attending more fairs?
Yes, definitely.

I loved picking out the colors to use on each cup.

75

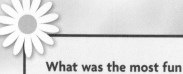

What was the most fun about the fair?
Getting to see everybody else's products. It was fun to see so many different kinds of crafts.

Were there other products at the fair that inspired you?
Yes. Someone was selling tie-dyed socks, and that made me think about doing something like that at home.

What was the least fun about the fair?
Having cups left over and having to pay back my parents for the supplies. I didn't make as much money as I thought I would.

Is there something special you want to buy with the money you make?
Some more sticker colors for my Cricut and some canvases for painting. And skin-care products.

There were so many creative products at the craft fair. It was very inspiring! These photos show just a few.

My dog, Frankie, likes to nap next to me while I craft.

Here I am weeding the stickers. That means taking off the unwanted material.

It was fun to talk to customers at the craft fair!

I'm a dog girl, just like Summer. Frankie is a goldendoodle.

What do you like about being your own boss?
Making the choices that I want to make. I didn't have to follow someone else's directions.

What advice would you give someone who wanted to start their own business?
Start off with something small and then move on to bigger ideas.

For Fiona, who wishes she had a dog
—C. H.

MEET THE **AUTHOR,** ILLUSTRATORS, AND ADVISERS

CLARE HUTTON grew up in Columbia, Maryland, with a dog, two cats, several goldfish, a hermit crab, and an older brother and sister. She now lives with her family in an apartment in Queens, New York, where, unfortunately, pets are not allowed, so she frequently borrows her friends' dogs. She has published many books for young readers, writing as both Clare Hutton and Clarissa Hutton.

MAIKE PLENZKE studied illustration at the Hamburg University of Applied Sciences Department of Design. She currently lives in Berlin with her partner and their dog. In her studio full of plants, Maike loves to create colorful illustrations for book covers, magazines, comic books, and other exciting projects.

ALLISON STEINFELD grew up in Connecticut, where she spent hours getting lost in library books. She currently lives in Atlanta, Georgia, with her two very fluffy cats. When not providing essential head scratches and belly rubs, she finds time to illustrate books like the Wait! What? series and the Kid Legends series.

KATIE FLORY works for the Maryland Society for the Prevention of Cruelty to Animals. In her current role as the Community Care and Advocacy Director, she analyzes and advocates for legislation affecting animal welfare. She also presents educational programs on animal safety and welfare to local schools and community groups. Katie lives with her three dogs, Rue, Gov. Tugg Boat Tank Speedman, and Buoy.

 JANEAR GARRUS is an educator and the founder of Chesapeake Educational Alliance (CHEDA), a company that creates and implements programming to enrich students in technology, digital media, and entrepreneurship. Through CHEDA, Janear directs and operates the Baltimore and Howard County Children's Business Fairs and Greater Purpose Christian Homeschoolers.

SUMMER'S STORY CONTINUES!

Will Crescent and Daphne get along? What's next for Waggy Pup Tails? Find out more in Summer's next book, coming in January 2025.

Visit **americangirl.com/play**
to discover more about Summer's world.

Look for bestselling books from
American Girl online and in stores.

Published by American Girl Publishing

24 25 26 27 28 29 30 QP 11 10 9 8 7 6 5 4 3 2

This book is a work of fiction. Any similarity to real persons, living or dead, is coincidental and not intended by American Girl. References to real events, people, or places are used fictitiously. Other names, characters, places, and incidents are the products of imagination.

All American Girl marks, Summer™, and Summer McKinny™ are trademarks of American Girl.

Written by Clare Hutton
Illustrations and cover image by Maike Plenzke
Doodle illustrations by Allison Steinfeld
Book design by Gretchen Becker
Editorial development by Teri Robida

Cataloging-in-Publication Data available from the Library of Congress

americangirl.com/service

Not all services are available in all countries.